Nothing had ever hurt so much in my life.

"Hey, Cindi," yelled Jodi. "You're the great skier. Come on! Show us your stuff!"

I wanted to make a great turn down to them. I pushed off hard with my poles.

I took off, but there were ridges in the snow.

Suddenly my ski slipped. I fell headfirst, and I started sliding down the mountain backwards, gaining speed. I knew I had to get my skies underneath me to stop the slide.

I twisted to right my balance. I felt my leg crack. I heard a snapping noise.

"It's broken! It's broken!" I screamed. I couldn't believe how much it hurt.

Look for these and other books in THE GYMNASTS series:

#1 *The Beginners*
#2 *First Meet*
#3 *Nobody's Perfect*
#4 *The Winner*
#5 *Trouble in the Gym*

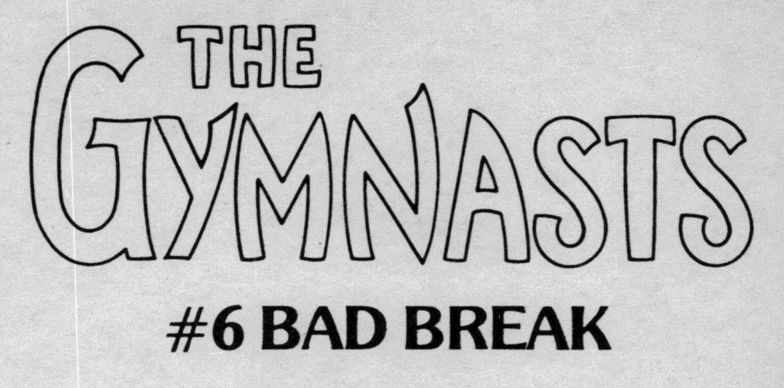

#6 BAD BREAK

Elizabeth Levy

AN
APPLE
PAPERBACK

SCHOLASTIC INC.
New York Toronto London Auckland Sydney

ISBN 0-590-42195-6

12 11 10 9 8 7 6 5 4 3 2 1 9/8 0 1 2 3 4/9

Printed in the U.S.A. 28

First Scholastic printing, July 1989

To Sukey, David, and Willie.
It's a lucky break you're my neighbors.

BAD BREAK

I Like Baby Mountains

"Cindi, it's easy," said Patrick. "Just do it and then we're done for the day."

"Do it," said Lauren, my best friend. "We can't leave for skiing if you spend the rest of your life on the beam."

I had been up on the beam for almost five minutes. I looked down at Patrick and the other Pinecones, who were waiting for me to finish my routine. The one good thing about being up on the beam is that you get to look down on everybody, even your coach. Patrick is my coach at the Evergreen Gymnastics Academy. The Pinecones are my team.

Patrick had just given us our new routine on

the beam. I thought our new beam routine was stupid. It wasn't that hard, but it had one move in it that I just couldn't get. It's called a Valdez back-walkover. It's a move that even little kids in gymnastics can do usually. It is just a back-bend starting from a sitting position. It's one thing to do a walkover on a solid floor, however, and another to do it on just four inches of beam with four feet of air below you.

I'm great on my floor exercise and on the uneven bars. I don't mind vaulting, but I hate being on the beam. Falling off the beam has been my problem ever since I started gymnastics.

Patrick consulted his clipboard. "Cindi," he said impatiently. "We're only halfway through the routine."

"Maybe I should do this another day," I said, still hesitating.

"How long do we have to wait for her?" whined Ashley. "It's my turn and we don't have much time left."

Ashley always whines. She's only nine, two years younger than me, but she's light-years ahead of me in whining.

"Ashley, don't bother her," said Ti An. "Cindi's concentrating." Ti An is even younger than Ashley. She's only eight. She's new to the Pinecones, and she takes gymnastics very seriously. I had to giggle. The truth was I wasn't really concentrating on the new routine; all I could think of was that I just had a few more minutes of gymnastics, and then my friends and I would be zooming away to the mountains for a long weekend of skiing.

Patrick glanced up at me. Sometimes I think he can read my mind. "Cindi, it's time to fish or cut bait. Are you going to do it, or do you want to try again next Tuesday?"

"Tuesday!" I said cheerfully. I hopped down. When Patrick gives me a choice, I take it. Most of the time Patrick just says, "DO IT!" But he must have sensed that my mind wasn't on gymnastics. In fact, I couldn't wait to get out of there. I was happy to have three days off the beam. I had a whole long weekend in front of me when I wouldn't have to think about school or gymnastics. All I had to think about was skiing and laughing.

My parents' friends had offered us the use of a huge house in Aspen for Washington's Birthday weekend. Aspen is only about a four-hour drive from where we live in Denver. We had been there before, but this was the first time I had been able to invite my own friends. I have a huge family, four brothers. I'm the baby of the family. Tim and Jared still live at home. Tim is sixteen, and he's my favorite. Jared is thirteen, and he's always on my case, although my friends like him. My two older brothers are at college.

My parents had allowed me to invite three friends to come to Aspen. Naturally, I had invited Lauren, Jodi, and Darlene, my three best friends at the Evergreen Gymnastics Academy. The four of us all started with Patrick at the same time. We think of ourselves as the original Pinecones.

Lauren Baca was my best friend even before gymnastics. We've been good friends since kindergarten, and we had begun tumbling together when we were in the first grade. But Lauren had quit gymnastics in third grade, and she would have given it up forever if it weren't for me.

Lauren and I met Darlene on our first day of gymnastics. We thought she was about sixteen and a model. It turns out that she's thirteen and just tall for her age. Darlene is intimidating when you first meet her because she is so beautiful, and her dad is famous. He's "Big Beef" Broderick, the linesman for the Denver Broncos. I believe that Darlene is the nicest of us all.

Jodi Sutton is a hoot. She is willing to try anything, including skiing, which she's done only a couple of times. But Jodi acts as if she's afraid of nothing. The weird thing is that she's not that great a gymnast, even though she comes from a whole family of gymnasts. Her mom is a coach at Patrick's gym, and her sister is a great gymnast, too. You'd think that Jodi would be ripe for the Olympics, but she's not. She's just not very coordinated. But I like her.

Jodi was the last one up on the beam. When she finished we'd be done for the day. Patrick glanced at his clipboard again. He hadn't memorized our new routine yet. "Jodi, here's where you curtsy," he said.

"Yes, your majesty," said Jodi as she dipped into a curtsy. Lauren and I giggled.

Jodi loves an audience. Unfortunately she dipped a little too far and started wobbling on the beam. "Whoa!" she said, trying to stop herself. She started laughing, and ended up falling off.

Patrick couldn't help laughing himself. "I can see the Pinecones are not in the mood for a new routine today," he said. "I know it's the start of a long weekend. I'll let you go. But I want to see all of you doing this new routine *soon.*"

"What will we get if we do it, your majesty?" asked Jodi, who was still laughing.

Patrick smiled. "I'll tell you what. When *all*, and I do mean *all*, the Pinecones get this routine, Pasta Patrick will make you a spaghetti dinner."

"All right!" I shouted. "Even I can stay on the

beam for that." Recently Patrick had learned to cook, and he had been telling us about his pasta creations. But he had never cooked for us.

"Cindi, it means you're going to have to nail that Valdez back-walkover."

"No problem," I said. "I'll be so loosey-goosey after my ski trip, I'll be able to do anything."

"Okay, loosey-goosey," said Patrick. "All you Pinecones come back in one piece. Have a good long weekend."

We rushed to the locker room. All our skis were stacked up in the corner, ready to go. I changed quickly. "I'm so excited!" said Jodi. "I can't wait."

"Me neither," said Darlene. "My mom got me the cutest hat. It's made out of fake leopard. I wouldn't wear real fur."

"You guys are so lucky," said Ti An. "I love to ski."

I felt a little bit guilty. It had never occurred to me to invite Ti An. But I couldn't invite everybody, and if I invited Ti An, I'd have to invite Ashley.

"I don't think gymnasts should ski," said Ashley. "It's too dangerous. I read somewhere that Bela Karolyi doesn't like his gymnasts to ski."

Bela Karolyi is just probably the world's most famous coach. He was born in Rumania, but he's got a school in Texas, and it seems that if you train with Karolyi, you end up in the Olympics. But we're not in his league.

"Where would they ski down in Texas, anyhow?" I asked. Ashley was a pain.

"It's the principle of the thing," said Ashley. "If you're a dedicated gymnast, you shouldn't risk injury doing another sport."

Jodi laughed. "Ashley, I think your brain got fried watching too much Olympics on television. You sound like one of those announcers."

"I'm just saying that I think you're being foolish," said Ashley. "Aren't I right, Becky?"

Ashley always looked to Becky to back her up. Becky Dyson is probably the best gymnast at the Academy, and she is definitely the most obnoxious. Luckily Becky is better than the Pinecones, so we don't have to work out with her.

"Whose skis are these?" complained Becky. She pushed them out of the way and they came tumbling down like a pile of pickup sticks.

"Hey!" I shouted. "Be careful! Those are expensive. Skis can break, you know."

Becky stepped over the skis without even considering picking them up. "They shouldn't be here anyhow. Somebody could get hurt," she said.

Lauren came to help me stack the skis back up against the wall.

"I wish one of them had bopped her on the head," whispered Lauren.

"Becky," repeated Ashley in her high squeaky voice, "don't you think it's true that gymnasts shouldn't ski? What if we got hurt?"

Becky looked at Ashley. "What *are* you talking about?" she asked. "I'm a great skier. I love to ski. I'm going skiing this weekend."

"See?" I said to Ashley. "You don't know what you're talking about."

"Skiing is great for coordination and balance," said Becky. "Of course, you have to be coordinated to begin with." She looked at me. "Your new routine is a cinch. Mine is a lot harder."

"So's your head," I mumbled.

I should have kept my mouth shut. I gave Becky an opening and she pounced. "What *were* you doing stuck up on the beam? Can't you do a simple walkover on the beam?"

"She's trying a *Valdez* walkover," said Lauren. Lauren won't let anybody put me down.

"I was doing that when I was nine," said Becky.

"I can do it," said Ashley. "You can, too, can't you, Ti An?"

Ti An looked at me and blushed. "Well, I can't do it very well," she said softly.

"I'll do it. Wait till Tuesday," I said, stuffing my leotard in my gym bag. I sometimes use my leotards as long underwear if it gets really cold when I'm skiing.

Darlene came dashing back into the locker room. "Cindi, they're here. Your brother's here to pick us up. Your folks are waiting for us at your house. I'm so psyched. I can't wait to get to Aspen. I hear they've got the cutest shops. The very first Esprit shop in the United States opened there."

Most people think of Aspen as a great place to ski. Trust Darlene to think of it as a great place to shop.

"Aspen!" shrieked Becky. "That's not where you Pinecones are going! I don't believe it!"

"What's wrong with Aspen?" I asked. I had visions of avalanches.

"Nothing's wrong with Aspen," said Becky. "Aspen is wonderful. That's why I'm going there. I was just looking forward to a weekend without Pinecones."

"We'll try to stay out of your way," I said. "It's a big ski slope."

"Not big enough," muttered Becky. "Who's going with you?"

"Lauren, Darlene, and Jodi," I answered.

"Darlene's not bad," said Becky.

"Me, I'm the worst skier," said Darlene. "Cindi's much better than I am."

"I didn't mean skier," said Becky, not elaborating on exactly what she did mean. But I knew. Becky and Darlene went to the same private school. The rest of us went to public school. Darlene doesn't have a snotty bone in her body, but Becky does. Darlene didn't even realize that Becky was being a snob.

"Where are you staying?" Becky asked.

"In a house," I answered. "It belongs to an airplane pilot friend of my dad's."

"Houses in Aspen are very expensive," said Becky. "It must be a little house."

"It's big enough for my whole family and the four original Pinecones. I've been there before. It looks right out on Buttermilk Mountain."

"Oh," said Becky. "Well, I rarely ski Buttermilk. It's for sissies. I like to ski Ajax. It's the big mountain."

"Big mountains for little brains," muttered Jodi.

I laughed a little nervously. Becky made me nervous. I know she's just a snob, and I shouldn't pay any attention to her, but she flusters me.

"I'm staying at the Hotel Jerome," said Becky. "Movie stars stay there."

"Great, a place to avoid," muttered Darlene. Becky could never really forgive Darlene for the fact that Darlene gets to meet celebrities all the time and she just doesn't care.

"Well, maybe I'll see you on the slopes," said Becky. "Which chair lifts do you take?"

"We ski all over," I answered.

Lauren gave me a worried look. Lauren hasn't skied as much as I have.

"Well, then I'm bound to see you," said Becky. "You can call me at the Jerome."

"If you call her, I'm not going," said Lauren after Becky left.

"We don't have to worry about her," I said. "As she said, it's a big ski slope."

"Is it big enough?" asked Lauren, who had never been to Aspen before.

"Wait till you see it," I said. "We can watch the skiers from the deck of the house where we're staying, and that's just on Buttermilk, 'the baby mountain,' as Becky would say."

"I like baby mountains," said Lauren. "I even like the sound of 'Buttermilk.' "

"You just like it 'cause it sounds like food," teased Jodi. "I want to go on the toughest mountain of them all."

"Jodi, you're from St. Louis," said Darlene.

"It's flat there. You've skied even less than me, and I'm not great."

"Yeah," said Jodi, "but I like a challenge."

"We'll stay away from any slope that has Becky," I said. "That will be challenge enough."

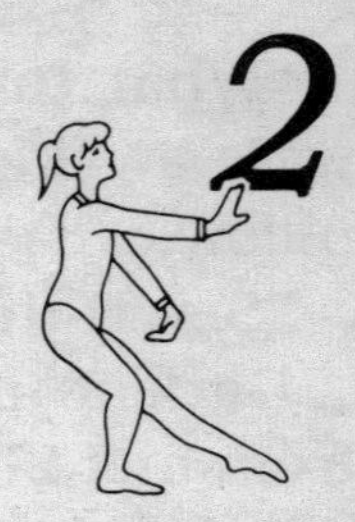

2

It's Not the End of the World

I woke up the next morning and I couldn't believe the mess we had made in just one night. All four of us were sleeping in one room with two bunk beds. The room looked like something from *Nightmare on Elm Street.* We had enough clothes strewn around to outfit an entire ski school, and most of them were Darlene's. I couldn't believe how much stuff she had brought for three days.

I looked out the window. At first it seemed gray, but then I looked up and realized the sky was blue. Our window was just shaded by the huge mountain across the ravine from our house on the edge of town.

"What time is it?" asked Darlene, sounding wide awake. Jodi's head was buried under her pillow.

"Seven-thirty," I answered.

Darlene popped out of the top bunk across from me. She was wearing a white cotton nightgown with a lace jacket. I was wearing a Grateful Dead T-shirt that used to belong to my brother.

"That shirt's cool," said Darlene. I felt proud. It wasn't often that Darlene admired anything that I owned.

"Grummmph," came a sound from the bunk below me.

"What's that sound?" asked Darlene. "A polar bear waking up?"

"I think it was Jodi," said Lauren, who was sleeping in the bunk below Darlene. "Either that or a polar bear got into our room."

"It's vacation time," grunted Jodi. "Why are we all up so early?"

"It's time to hit the slopes," I said. I could already smell the bacon cooking in the upstairs kitchen. Mom is fanatical about our health and Dad's cholesterol, except when we go skiing. Then she goes back to believing that we all need a huge breakfast.

"I've got to get dressed," said Darlene.

"How many outfits did you bring?" I asked. I

had one pair of ski pants that fit over my ski boots. They're out of style. I knew Darlene would have the latest.

She did, of course. She had a bright yellow powder jumpsuit. It was so bright it was like having a neon light in the room.

"At least we won't lose you on the slopes," I said.

"Do you think it'll be cold enough to wear my fake leopard hat?" she asked.

"For breakfast?" Lauren asked. "I think you'll be overdressed."

Darlene threw her hat at Lauren. We looked at Jodi's bunk. She was still lying with her head under the pillow.

We pounced on her. She got up quickly. "All right . . . all right," said Jodi.

"Pinecones don't sleep away their vacation," said Lauren.

"Pinecones can try, can't they," grunted Jodi.

Upstairs, Tim was mixing the pancake batter. I love vacations. Darlene offered to set the table. Jared jumped up to help her. I think Jared has a little bit of a crush on Darlene, and it isn't just because he's in awe of Darlene's dad.

"Where are you skiing?" Jared asked.

"Buttermilk," I answered. I knew that Jared would want to ski Ajax Mountain. "I don't think

Lauren, Jodi, and Darlene are ready for Ajax."

"Thanks," said Darlene. I thought she was being sarcastic.

"I didn't mean that as a put-down," I said quickly. "It's just that I've been skiing since I've been six."

"Hey," said Darlene. "I meant thanks for real. I don't want to go down Ajax. But we don't have to stick together like glue."

"What exactly am I not up to?" Jodi asked.

"Schussing down the tough mountain," teased Jared.

"I am *too* tough enough!" said Jodi defensively.

"I think I'll ski with you guys," said Jared.

"Girls," I said. "We're girls, not boys. I'm not sure we want you. I think we'll have to vote on it."

Jared looked hurt.

"I'll vote yes," said Darlene.

I had been looking forward to taking the Pinecones out by myself. I was the best skier of the four of us, and I liked the idea of being the leader. But Jared was at least as good as I was, if not better.

Tim started making pancakes, and by the time we finished breakfast I was so anxious to get going that I didn't mind Jared tagging along.

It was a beautiful, sunny day. Perfect for

skiing. Mom and Dad dropped us off at Buttermilk and went to ski Ajax. Tim decided to do a few practice runs on Buttermilk, too.

We got our tickets for the chair lift. I put on my goggles. Lauren stood beside me. I saw her looking up the mountain and the skiers schussing down the slopes.

"Are you sure this is the baby mountain?" she asked.

"Don't be fooled by the skiers speeding by," I said. "It's an intermediate slope. Everybody just likes to show off here 'cause it's easy."

"Look at that turkey," said Darlene. "She's sliding down the whole mountain."

I looked to where Darlene was pointing. Someone was skiing totally out of control. The skier came closer to the bottom of the slope, and it looked like she wouldn't be able to stop colliding with those of us standing in the line. She tried to do a snowplow to stop, but she couldn't even do that.

I started to grab Lauren's arm to pull her out of the way when I heard a voice yell, "Yoo-hoo! I thought it was you."

The skier removed her goggles.

"Becky!" I exclaimed. I giggled. I couldn't believe what a lousy skier she was.

"Hi, guys," she said.

"What are you doing here?" I asked.

Becky pretended not to understand my question. "I told you I was going to be in Aspen."

"Yes, but you said you liked to ski Ajax, the tough mountain," I reminded her.

Becky didn't even blush. It's impossible to embarrass that girl. "I wanted a few easy runs to sharpen my skills," she said. "I'll even ski a run with you."

She was like the queen offering crumbs to the peasants. I really didn't want Becky hanging around with us. She would spoil our fun. But getting rid of her wasn't going to be so easy.

"Uhh, we're going to take it slow," I said. "It's our first run. We may be too boring for you."

Jodi guffawed. "I won't be," she said.

I poked Jodi in the ribs. Jodi stared at me and then realized that I was just trying to get free of Becky.

"Cindi's right," said Jodi quickly. "We'll be too slow for you. Lauren's just learning."

"Me?" protested Lauren. "I'm better than you are. It's Darlene who's the slowest. She has to make perfect slow turns so that everyone can admire her outfit."

I had to laugh. You might be able to take gymnasts out of the gym, but you sure couldn't take the competitiveness out of the gymnasts. Here we were just in line for the chair lift, and everyone was bragging about how good they could ski.

I smiled to myself, because — just this once — I didn't have to brag. I was the best. It wasn't like gymnastics. Darlene is always better than me on the beam. On any given day, if she hits her routine, Jodi can be as good as me on the uneven bars. No one can beat Lauren on vault when she's hot. We were all about even in gymnastics. That's why we were Pinecones, and that's why Becky wasn't. Because Becky was better than any of us.

But at skiing, I was the best. I had been doing it longer than any of the others, and I was genuinely good. From what I had seen of Becky's trip down the mountain, I was way better than she was.

We moved up the line for the chair. Jared maneuvered himself so that he and Darlene went together.

The operator motioned for the next two. Lauren and Jodi were in front of me. I nudged them.

Lauren hesitated. "That leaves you with Becky," she whispered. "Sorry."

"It's not the end of the world," I said.

I was almost wrong.

3

I Screamed!

Becky almost dropped her ski pole as we were getting on the chair lift. It clanged against the center pole. I was able to spear it with my own pole and haul it back in toward the chair like a caught fish. It was a pretty nifty catch, if I say so myself. Becky didn't thank me, naturally.

I put down the safety bar and settled into the chair. Becky's mittened hands were caked with snow and so was her hat. That only happens when you've taken a few bad spills. I wondered how many times Becky had fallen coming down the mountain.

"It looks like you picked up most of the mountain as you were coming down," I joked.

"The first run was just to get the kinks out," said Becky. "Now I'm ready to fly. I probably won't stay with you guys for very long. I don't like to be slowed down."

I thought about the snowplow stop I had seen her do near the chair lift. No way were the Pinecones going to slow Becky down. It tickled me to think that Becky was such a liar. She had sounded like such an ace skier back at the gym, but she was just a beginner.

"How long have you been skiing?" I asked her innocently.

Becky turned her blue eyes on me. "I didn't have time for it until last year. Gymnastics kept me busy. But then I came out here on spring break, and I took a few lessons. The instructor said I was amazingly coordinated. Of course, that's because of my gymnastics skills. My instructor said I picked skiing up faster than any student he had ever had."

Becky rambled on and on. I couldn't stop her. She was so boring. Becky had only two subjects that interested her — bragging about herself or putting down someone else.

I leaned over the safety bar to watch the skiers coming down the mountain.

"What are you doing?" Becky shrieked. "You're rocking the chair. We'll fall out!"

I hadn't rocked the chair and the safety bar was down. We couldn't possibly fall out of the chair.

"I was just looking down there to see if I could spot my brother Tim." Tim was always easy to spot because he wore a bright red parka.

I saw a dot of red moving down the mountain with a beautiful, smooth rhythm. He was going down the fall line, the steepest part of the mountain, but he was totally in control.

"Go, TIMMY!" I shouted into the wind. Timmy skidded to a stop and waved his ski pole at me.

"Do you know that skier?" asked Becky. "He looks like he belongs in the Olympics."

"He's my brother," I said.

"He's good," Becky said.

"I usually ski with him," I added.

"Can you go down that part of the mountain?" Becky asked.

I grinned at her. "I thought you skied Ajax. This part of the mountain's easy. Let's take it when we get to the top."

I thought I saw Becky turn a little bit pale. I loved being able to get her scared, and the great thing was that I would be able to pull it off. The run that Tim had just gone down would be no trouble for me, and the rest of the Pinecones could handle it. I couldn't wait.

We pulled up close to the top. I could see Darlene and Jared already off their chair and waiting for us a little way down the mountain.

Lauren and Jodi turned around to wave at me. I gave them a little wave, but I wanted them to turn around and face front again so that they could get off the chair without any trouble. I remembered one ride with Lauren when she had forgotten to take her poles off the hook and her poles rode the chair lift back down the mountain. I had to lend her mine, because it was easier for me to ski without poles than it was for her.

"Take your poles," I said to Becky, as I started to lift the safety bar.

The chair made the little bumping noise it always did when we were at the top. Becky had to get off first before I could get off. She swung her pole around and almost hit me in the eye. I was going to be lucky if I got out of the chair alive.

Finally I had to half push her out of the chair to get myself out on time.

Becky flung herself around to ask me what I was doing. "Move over!" I yelled. "I need some room."

"Cindi, you're such a nerd," said Becky as she straightened her mittens and hat.

"Becky, we have to get out of the way of the other skiers," I warned her. The two skiers behind us were just getting off the chair lift, and we were directly in their way.

"Get out of the way!" I yelled at Becky.

I gave her a little push. Her skis crossed. I could see she was going to fall. I had my poles in one hand. I reached out my free hand to help steady Becky.

She got her tips free and started to slide down the hill toward Jodi, Darlene, Lauren, and Jared.

I looked down at them. They were laughing. I started to laugh, too.

"Hey, Cindi," yelled Jodi. "You're the great skier. Come on! Show us your stuff!"

I wanted to make a super turn down to them. I pushed off hard with my poles.

I took off, but there were ridges in the snow.

Suddenly my ski slipped. I fell headfirst, and I started sliding down the mountain backwards, gaining speed. I knew I had to get my skies underneath me to stop the slide.

I twisted to right my balance. I felt my leg crack. I heard a snapping noise.

I screamed.

Nothing had ever hurt so much in my life.

4

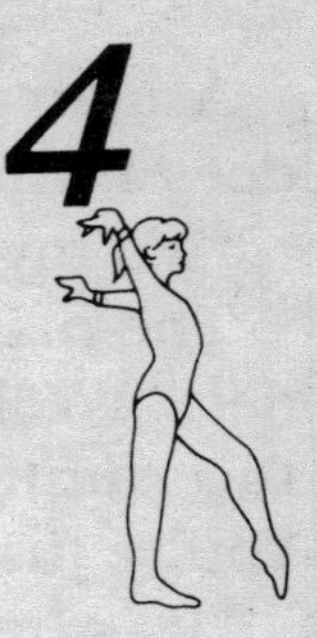

I'm Not Brave. I'm Scared!

I couldn't believe how much it hurt. I knew my leg was broken.

"It's broken! It's broken!" I screamed. I could see Becky's terrified face staring down at me, her mouth a big O. I didn't want her there.

"Cindi, Cindi!" I heard Jared yell. Within seconds, Darlene, Jodi, and Lauren were all standing over me. I stuck my mittened hand in my mouth to try to stop myself from screaming.

I looked up. Jared was crouched next to me. Darlene, Jodi, and Lauren were holding their hands to their mouths.

A stranger pushed my friends to the side. "Give her room, give her room," said the voice.

A man with a beard leaned over me. "Where does it hurt?" he asked.

"It's my leg. It's broken. It's broken!" I cried.

The man put a reassuring hand on my shoulder. "We'll get a ski patrol sled to take you down to examine your leg. It probably isn't broken. You're just scared."

"It *is* broken! It's broken!" I yelled. "I heard it! I know."

"There, there," he said. "You can't know that until we get some experts to take some pictures. Lots of kids think they broke their leg, and it's only fear."

"He's right!" Becky said. "Cindi's probably not hurt very bad."

The man patted my shoulder patronizingly, as if he thought I was hysterical.

I wanted to bite his hand. He made me furious.

"Cindi doesn't usually scream," I heard Jared say in a scared voice. "Cindi can take a lot of pain."

"I can't! I can't!" I sniffled, a little embarrassed that I was so out of control, but my leg throbbed so much.

"Cindi, you'll be okay," Lauren whispered. Her face looked like a little white oval under her ski hat. She looked more scared than I was. I think she was crying.

Two other ski patrollers brought a sled next to me. "Where's she hurt?" one of the patrollers asked.

"It's her leg," said the man. "She thinks she broke it."

"If she thinks it's broken it probably is," said the ski patrolwoman. She knelt down beside me.

"Does it hurt much?" she asked.

I nodded. Just the fact that she believed me when I said my leg was broken made me feel better.

"Does anybody know this girl?" the patroller asked.

"I do!" shouted Darlene.

"I do, too!" yelled Jodi and Lauren together.

"She's my sister!" yelled Jared.

"I know her . . . sort of . . . ," mumbled Becky.

The ski patrolwoman patted my shoulder. "It sounds like you've got a lot of friends. Okay, let's get this leg in a splint and get her out of here."

They put on a plastic leg splint with Velcro straps.

Quickly, hands were underneath me, and the next thing I knew I was wrapped like a mummy in a blanket and placed in the sled. The ski patrolwoman pulled at a strap across my chest.

"We have to make this tight," she said. "I'm sorry if it's uncomfortable. What's your name?"

“Cindi,” I sniffled.

“Cindi, my name is Ann. I’ll be with you all the way to the bottom.”

“Hi, Ann,” I managed to whisper, but I wasn’t really in the mood for much chitchat.

“Well, Cindi, you’re pretty courageous. I’ve seen adults twice your age, screaming and crying in fear. I haven’t seen one tear from you.”

“She’s a gymnast,” I heard Jodi say. Jodi was leaning over the sled.

“Is that a fact?” said the ski patrolwoman. “Maybe that accounts for why you’re so brave.”

I didn’t feel brave. I wondered if they realized I wasn’t screaming because I was too terrified.

I swallowed hard. I suddenly felt as if I were dying of thirst. Fear must make you thirsty.

“We have to take you down the mountain in the sled. I’ll be in front. Steven will be in back,” said Ann. “It’ll be frightening, because you may think that we’re out of control, but we will be going slower than it feels. There’s no danger. Your leg is secure.”

“We haven’t lost a customer yet,” joked the bearded ski patrolman.

I had seen injured skiers being brought down on a sled. It looked petrifying.

Ann took the lead. I was right to be terrified.

The sound of the steel edges of her skis biting into the snow and ice as she tried to control the sled will be with me all my life. It wasn't a smooth swish, the swish that you hear when you're skiing. It sounded like a buzz saw trying to cut through concrete. The ride seemed to take forever because whenever they came to a bump, they skidded to a stop and lifted my sled over the bump.

People tell you that when something awful happens to you, you go into shock and don't remember it. I remember it all. I couldn't see much. The blanket kept covering my eyes. The snow seeped in through the cracks in the blanket, and the noise . . . the noise was almost worse than the pain.

I never knew where we were. I didn't know how much farther we had to go to get down the mountain. It seemed to take forever.

Finally the sled stopped. Ann took the blanket away from my face. My hands were tied down by the strap across my chest. I was helpless.

"You're such a brave kid," said Ann. I blinked the snow away from my eyes. I shook my head, trying to tell her that it wasn't courage; it was terror.

They transferred me to an ambulance to take

me to the hospital. "Where's my brother?" I cried. "And Mom and Dad! And my friends? I can't go without them."

"Your brother and your friends are looking for your parents," said Ann. "They'll find them, and they'll all meet you at the hospital."

"Are you coming with me?" I asked.

"No," said Ann. "But the ambulance crew will take good care of you. The hospital is close to the slopes. It's only a short ride. You'll be fine."

I wasn't. My leg started throbbing even worse than before. I think the terror of the sled ride had made me forget momentarily how much my leg was hurting.

The doors to the ambulance closed with a clang. The siren went on with a short burst. We started to move. I was terrified. I hated that ambulance drive.

If only I could have had something in my ears to drown out the pain and fear. If I ever get rich, I'm going to endow every ambulance with a Walkman and some tapes.

When we reached the hospital, they wheeled me out of the ambulance, and I didn't see Mom or Dad or Lauren or anybody. I was really afraid.

I didn't have any of the numbers the hospital wanted, like for Blue Cross/Blue Shield.

It wasn't a horror story. The nurses and doctors and the workers at the hospital weren't mean or anything, but I felt so alone. I wanted Mom and Dad to be with me so much! Or even Jared! I got mad at the Pinecones for leaving me. I was mad at everybody, I was alone, and I was scared.

Then someone gave me a shot and everything became a little bit fuzzier. I liked things fuzzier.

5

Don't Let Them See You Cry

I was never completely unconscious, but the edge was off the pain. It was like I was there, but I wasn't. The next thing I remember was Mom holding my hand while someone wrapped wet bandages around my leg from my hip to my toe. The very next moment the bandages turned to stone, and I was in a fiberglass cast. I remember that Mom didn't even take the time to take off her ski boots.

As they were wheeling me down the hospital corridor, Mom's boots made a funny metallic sound. It's strange how I remember the sounds most of all.

Mom stayed with me all night, sleeping in the empty bed in my room. I guess even in the ski season, Aspen is a pretty healthy place. The hospital didn't seem crowded. In the morning, Jodi, Darlene, Lauren, Jared, and Dad all came to see me in my hospital room. The room was actually pretty with a window overlooking the ski slopes on Buttermilk, just like the room in our house. I didn't care how pretty it was. I wanted to get out of there.

I was actually a little giddy from the medication they gave me for the pain.

Darlene walked into the room and burst out crying. She started a chain reaction. Tears came to Lauren's eyes and even Jodi started sniffling. I half expected Jodi to crack a joke. But she looked at me, and then at the cast on my leg, and her face just kind of crumbled.

I was the only dry-eyed one in the place, and it was my leg that was broken.

"Hey, gang," I said. "It's a broken leg, not World War III. Could you stop the tear ducts? I could drown in here." There was a knock on the door. A doctor walked into a mob scene of people crying. The only calm one was me, the patient. The doctor was carrying a brand-new pair of crutches.

Mom quickly dug into her knapsack for a package of Kleenex and handed them around the room.

The doctor looked at my chart. "Are you Cindi?"

"I'm the one with the broken leg." I pointed to the cast.

Jodi laughed as if I had just said the funniest joke in the world.

"We're the Jocketts," said Dad, standing up.

The doctor looked around at the crowd in my room. "All of you?" he asked. He seemed puzzled, and I don't blame him.

He must have thought we were one big adopted family, the kind you read about in *People* magazine. Lauren's half Hispanic, Darlene's black, Jodi's a blonde, and I'm a strawberry blonde. I never thought of it before, but if you add Ti An, who's Vietnamese, we Pinecones are our own mini United Nations. Maybe we could form a rock group like UB40.

"Not all of us are Jocketts," I said. "Some of us are Pinecones. Me, I'm a Pinecone and a Jockett."

The doctor didn't look amused.

Dad asked the doctor about my leg.

"She's lucky," said the doctor.

"Lucky!" exclaimed Lauren.

Mom hushed Lauren. She wanted to hear what the doctor had to say.

"Lucky because it's a clean break. She broke the tibia, which is one of the strongest bones in the body. It's the long bone that runs along the shin. I've brought you a copy of her X rays so that you can take them home to your regular doctor."

"Oh, goody, a souvenir," I said. "I'll put it up next to my picture of Greg Louganis, the diver."

The doctor looked as if he preferred patients who didn't speak.

He turned back to my parents. "I don't know how she did it. She must have been skiing very fast."

"She was practically standing still," exclaimed Jared.

The doctor shrugged. "Then it was just one of those freak accidents. She must have twisted as she fell and applied all her weight on the bone. These things happen. The important thing is that we won't have to operate to reset it. The neighboring muscles and other tissues were undamaged. It should mend in about six to eight weeks."

I was lying there half asleep with my tongue

between my teeth. Suddenly I clamped down with my jaw. I jerked as I bit my tongue.

Mom squeezed my hand.

"Two months!" I croaked. "I can't be out of gymnastics for two months."

The doctor laughed as if I had finally made a very funny joke, but I wasn't being funny. I couldn't imagine being immobile for that long. I'd never be able to catch up in gymnastics. It was ridiculous. I wasn't even in much pain.

The doctor came over to the bed. "Well, I'm afraid you'll have to live with it, but we'll have a physical therapist come in and get you moving again."

He examined my toes, which were sticking out of the cast. "Good," he said.

"What's good about my toes?" I asked.

"They aren't turning blue. That's why we kept you in the hospital overnight, to make sure there wasn't swelling."

"How would you know what's going on under this cast?" I asked.

"Believe me," said the doctor. "We'd know. Your toes would turn color, and you'd feel the pain."

"What would have happened if there was swelling?" I wanted to know.

"We would have had to break the cast and put on a new one," said the doctor. I winced at the word "break."

"Now I'm going to have the physical therapist give you a lesson on using your crutches. As soon as she says you can walk on the crutches, you can leave."

"We should have brought Becky," said Darlene. "She would have loved teaching you."

Becky had once had a badly sprained ankle, and they put her in a walking cast for a few weeks. She had acted as if it was the injury of the century.

"Where *is* Becky?" I asked.

Jodi looked out the window and pointed to the ski slope. "She's skiing. She should have a warning sign on her parka. 'Bad Luck.' "

"She did call this morning. She said she was worried about you," said Darlene.

"I'm glad she's not here," I muttered. I had no desire to see Becky.

A woman came into the room carrying a small riser of two steps. "Excuse me," she said impatiently. "I would like you to clear the room of everyone but Cindi's parents."

Lauren, Jodi, and Darlene didn't want to leave, but Mom shooed them out.

The physical therapist helped me sit up. My leg felt so strange dangling from the bed. It hurt, but it somehow didn't feel connected to me.

"Just stay in a sitting position for a minute," said the therapist. "You've been prone for almost twenty-four hours."

I couldn't believe that an entire day had passed. My whole life had changed in just a split second. If I hadn't run into Becky . . . if Jodi hadn't shouted to me . . . if I hadn't been so stupid to try to show off, it would never have happened.

"Will she have to use stairs when she's at home?" the therapist asked my parents.

Dad nodded. "Her bedroom's on the second floor. But she can sleep in the living room."

The therapist shook her head. "No, it's better if the patient uses stairs. The more she moves her leg, even in the cast, the faster it will heal. As soon as she masters the crutches, she's free to go home."

I felt like raising my hand to remind the therapist that "she" was in the room. She talked to Mom and Dad as if Cindi, the patient, wasn't there. She made me very mad.

Finally she spoke to me. "Make sure the crutches are firmly in front of you before you shift your weight," she said as she handed me the crutches.

I stood up for the first time since the accident. I didn't feel dizzy. I stuck the crutches under my armpits. They were the right size.

I hopped up and down the length of the room. Every time my leg jiggled it sent little shock waves of pain all the way up to my armpits. I was sweating, but I didn't want to tell the snooty therapist that it hurt.

"Try going up the steps," she said. "The trick is to always keep your weight behind you."

It was like learning a new trick in gymnastics. I took the two steps easily.

The doctor came back in the room and watched my progress. He was frowning, and I thought I was doing something wrong. "Has she broken a leg before?" he asked.

"No, I haven't," I snapped.

"Most people don't pick up how to balance on the crutches so quickly." He sounded as if I were a medical freak.

"Cindi's a gymnast," said Mom, giving me back my name. "She's very coordinated."

"Well, that explains it," said the doctor, standing up. "I'm sure she'll mend very quickly. Young people do. In two months, she'll be as good as new."

Two months! I looked down at my cast. Two months. I had never taken off from gymnastics for two months. Two months would be like two years.

I wanted to cry, but I didn't. I wouldn't give the doctor the satisfaction of seeing me cry.

6

Life Stinks

When we had arrived in Aspen I thought our room had looked like *Nightmare on Elm Street*. Maybe we had gone to a movie, *Nightmare in Aspen*, and soon the lights would go up and I would find out that I had never gotten on a chair lift with Becky, and that none of this had ever happened.

But it wasn't a nightmare, and the cast was going home with me. I finally got to leave the hospital that afternoon. I felt awful that I had ruined everybody's vacation even though Darlene kept saying she was glad of an excuse not to have to ski.

"Besides," said Jodi, "if anybody's to blame, I am. If I hadn't shouted to you at that moment, it would never have happened."

I couldn't believe what Jodi was saying. "It's not your fault," I said quickly, but I could tell from her face that I really wasn't making her feel better.

"I mean it," I repeated it.

Jodi just looked away. It was so unlike Jodi to feel guilty. Jodi usually just barrels straight ahead and doesn't worry. Now I felt guilty for making her feel guilty.

"When do we get to sign your cast?" asked Lauren. "I think we should be the first since we were at the scene of the accident."

I looked down at the huge white chunk of a cast. I felt the ridges of the plastic. Somehow I didn't want it decorated with cute little hearts and sayings.

"Uh . . . these casts are hard to draw on," I said.

"We got Magic Markers," said Darlene. "We got them in all different colors."

"NO!" I shouted louder than I expected.

My friends looked shocked.

My leg still hurt. I didn't want anybody to touch my cast.

I tried to make a joke out of it. "It's my fashion

statement. Plain casts are in this year. Right, Darlene?"

Darlene always complained that I had no fashion sense.

Darlene didn't laugh. "Why don't you want us to sign it?" she asked seriously.

I shrugged. At least I could still move my shoulders. "I just don't want it signed, okay?"

Everyone looked a little bit hurt, but I couldn't help myself. Everyone seemed so depressed. I couldn't stand it. I felt it was all my fault that everyone was so down.

We left Aspen early because Mom and Dad wanted to get home before dark. I rode stretched out in the way-back of the station wagon, surrounded by pillows.

"This is the life," I joked, trying to lighten the atmosphere. Lauren, Jodi, Darlene, and Jared had to sit squashed in the backseat. "Are you guys okay?"

"We're fine," muttered Jared.

"It's too bad we didn't fly to Aspen," I said.

"Why?" asked Darlene, turning in her seat so that she could see me.

" 'Cause when they announce, 'Does anyone need assistance?' I could have been the first one up on the plane. That would be cool. It would make breaking my leg worth it."

"That's sick," said Lauren.

"Hey, Dad!" I shouted. "You've got to take me with you on a trip so that I can fly with my cast." Dad's an airplane pilot, and I get to go on lots of trips with him.

Darlene stared at me. "What's wrong?" I asked.

"How can you keep making jokes?" asked Darlene.

"I like jokes," I said. "What do you want me to do, whine and cry?"

"Everybody's cried but you," said Darlene.

"Well, I'm sorry," I snapped. Darlene made it sound as if something was wrong with me because I hadn't cried. "I'm sure I'll cry when you all go back to gymnastics, and I'm stuck at home. You all will have learned the new routines and be eating pasta. I'll be eating dirt."

"I'm sure Patrick will invite you to our pasta dinner," said Darlene.

"Thanks," I muttered. "I don't want any special favors."

"You're in a great mood," said Lauren sarcastically.

"Excuse me," I said. "I just broke my leg. I'll try to cheer up. Anyone know any good knock-knock jokes?" I asked. Then I actually remembered a good one.

"Knock, knock," I said.

"Who's there," answered Lauren, but she didn't sound like her heart was in it.

"Eileen," I answered.

"Eileen who?" asked Jodi. At least she sounded a little more jolly than Lauren or Darlene. My friends were turning my broken leg into a great tragedy. I didn't want their pity.

"Eileen Dover and fell down," I said, cracking up.

Darlene groaned. "Cindi, that's not funny."

"It is funny. You guys are a real drag," I said. "How come you don't know any broken-bone jokes?"

"Honey, why don't you just try to rest?" asked Mom.

"I've got nothing to do but rest," I said crankily. "I'll be dragging this stupid cast around for a long time."

"You'll be able to do things," said Mom. "We'll rent lots of movies."

"Great," I muttered.

"We'll come over to visit you every day," said Lauren.

"You'll be at gymnastics," I snapped. "You're all Pinecones. Patrick will probably kill me for breaking my leg."

Jodi giggled.

"What's so funny?" I asked.

"Nothing," giggled Jodi. "It's just that I don't think Patrick will kill you. He'll feel bad." Jodi giggled again.

Jodi was giggling just because she was nervous. I knew Jodi thought it was her fault. Maybe I should have tried to say something else to make her feel better, but I felt pretty lousy myself.

We didn't joke much the rest of the way home, but I didn't sleep, either. My leg was hurting. My friends were feeling guilty. Life stunk.

Everyone Knows Best . . . But Me

The day after I got home, I had to be checked out by my own doctor, Dr. Heilbrun. I like Dr. Heilbrun. She never talks about me in the third person. Even when I was a real little kid she treated me as if I could understand what was happening to me.

"What a bad break!" said Dr. Heilbrun when she saw me in the cast. "It's not going to be easy for such an active kid like you to be in a cast."

"You're telling *me*," I answered.

"A break is a real shock to your system," said Dr. Heilbrun.

I shrugged. "Lots of people get broken legs. It happens in gymnastics all the time."

"But it's never happened to you," said Dr. Heilbrun. "You've never had a broken bone before."

"I know," I muttered.

"It's a clean break," said Dr. Heilbrun.

"That's what the doctor in Aspen said." I wished I knew what a clean break meant. I had a million questions, but somehow I couldn't ask them. I was almost scared to ask them. Some of my questions were so stupid. Would the leg out of the cast grow while the leg in the cast didn't? Would I end up walking with a limp?

"I think you need some time to recuperate," said Dr. Heilbrun, after she X-rayed my leg. "Would you like to take the rest of the week off?"

"No, I'm bored," I said. "I want to go back to school. And I don't want to miss much class work."

Dr. Heilbrun put her arm around my shoulders. "Cindi, you are a strong kid. It's just like you to want to get right back. If you feel like it, I'll tell your mother you can go to school tomorrow. And I know you'll want to keep up your strength for gymnastics. I can give you a booklet of exercises that you can do. Do you have any small weights at home? You can do some hand and arm exercises."

I shook my head no.

"I'll talk to your mom about getting some," said

Dr. Heilbrun. "We'll keep you in shape."

"Great," I said with a smile. But I didn't feel so great. My leg still hurt. It wasn't shooting pain anymore, but it was almost a constant ache.

"When your brother Tim broke his leg, he complained the whole time," said Dr. Heilbrun.

"Gymnasts are tougher than football players," I bragged.

Dr. Heilbrun laughed. "Well, don't be too tough. Take care of yourself. It won't be easy. Does your leg ache a lot?"

"A little," I admitted.

"In a short while, your leg will start to itch. There's nothing we can do about it. I've seen kids do crazy things . . . stick coat hangers down their casts, try to pour baby powder into their casts. All of those things only make it worse. Promise me you'll just grin and bear it."

"I will," I said. "What choice do I have?" Dr. Heilbrun laughed as if I were making a joke, but I wasn't joking. I was depressed. I felt like a prisoner.

On the way back home, Mom stopped at the mall so I could pick up a couple of movies. The Evergreen Mall is right down the road from the Evergreen Gymnastics Academy.

"Do you want to stop in and say hello to Patrick?" Mom asked.

I shook my head. "He'll be busy," I mumbled.

"He might be free. I'm sure he'll want to see you."

"Mom," I whined, "my leg's hurting. I'm really not in the mood."

I was quickly learning that "my leg's hurting" were the magic words that could let me get my own way. But I just wasn't in the mood to see Patrick.

I rented *Little Shop of Horrors*. It was perfect. Funny and not too scary, but I wasn't really concentrating on the movie. My leg did hurt, and I was lonely. Everyone was being very nice. Mom had put an ice bucket next to me and a six-pack of sodas. She was even letting me munch on Cheetos, my favorite junk food, but it wasn't much fun.

I heard the doorbell ring.

"Cindi," Mom yelled, "somebody's here to see you."

I looked up. Patrick was standing in the doorway.

"What are *you* doing here?" I exclaimed, grabbing for my crutches and trying to stand up. I knocked over the can of soda next to my toes. I tried to hop out of the way. I had visions of sticky soda being on my cast forever.

Mom ran into the kitchen to get a towel.

"Sorry," I muttered to Patrick. "I'm sort of dangerous to be around with my crutches and cast."

Patrick took the towel from Mom and helped wipe up the soda. "Sit down, Cindi," he said, "before you do any more damage."

I laughed. At least Patrick sounded as if he was treating me normally. I was getting sick of the half-sad voice I heard from Mom all day. It's no fun being around someone who feels sorry for you all the time.

"Patrick, you won't believe how brave Cindi's been," said Mom. "I don't think she cried once."

"That's Cindi," said Patrick. He sounded proud of me.

"I just found out about your accident," he said. "I wanted to see for myself how you were doing."

"It was such a stupid way to break my leg," I said. "At least I could have been doing something glamorous, like when Becky hurt herself doing the Eagle."

"Becky had a sprain. You've got a broken leg," said Patrick.

"I know," I said. "I'm sorry." I was a little worried that Patrick would be mad at me for hurting myself doing something other than gymnastics. I remembered Ashley saying that Bela Karolyi wouldn't let his gymnasts go skiing. I knew that Patrick admired Karolyi.

Patrick grinned at me. "What are you saying you're sorry for, sport? It was an accident. Accidents happen."

"It was such a wimpy way to break my leg," I admitted. "I wasn't even really skiing hard. I was just getting off the chair lift."

Patrick laughed. He looked up at my mother. "Did you raise your daughter to think she had to be Wonder Woman?"

"I think it was growing up with four brothers," said Mom. "It turned her into a macho kid."

"Who's macho?" I protested. "I'm not!"

Patrick ruffled my hair. "Okay, Iron Woman, when can I expect you back in the gym?"

I looked down at my cast. "It'll be weeks at least before this comes off," I said. "I'll miss you, though. I won't be learning the new routines for a long time. I'll miss your pasta dinner."

Patrick frowned at me. "I don't want you staying away from the gym for two months," he said.

I laughed. "Well, I'm going back to school tomorrow, but I think it'll be a little bit longer before I'm ready to go back up on the beam."

"I wasn't talking about going up on the beam," said Patrick, "but you're still part of the Pinecones. You can help me keep records. And then I'd like to talk to your doctor about what you can do to keep in shape. We have an ergometric bike at the gym. You can use it with just one leg. Your leg's broken, but there's no reason we can't work on your upper body and the other leg."

"That's a great idea," said Mom, enthusiastically. "We just went to see Dr. Heilbrun today, and she recommended that Cindi do work with some light weights. I was going to buy some."

"I'd rather have Cindi come to the gym," said Patrick. "I have some lightweight dumbbells and other weights. In fact, I'll give Cindi's doctor a call and set up a specific program."

Mom and Patrick sounded so eager and excited, but it was just like in the hospital. Everyone was talking about Cindi as if I weren't there. I gazed down at my cast. I wondered why having one leg in a cast made me invisible. It was weird. Nobody was asking my opinion anymore. Everybody knew what was best for Cindi and her leg. Everybody except me. I had my doubts — lots of them — but nobody cared.

8

This Isn't So Bad After All

On Monday, just a week after my accident, I swung into the Evergreen Gymnastics Academy on my crutches. Jodi, Darlene, and Lauren were at my side like bodyguards. People think you hobble when you have a broken leg, but you really don't. Walking on crutches is a swinging motion, and it takes as much strength as swinging from the bars. In just one week I could feel the difference in my arms. I tried to concentrate on not using my armpits, and making my biceps carry my weight.

"I'm so glad you're coming back," said Lauren. "We missed you."

"Yeah," said Jodi. "It didn't seem like the old Pinecones with you not there. Ashley's getting out of hand without you to put her in her place. Now that you're back, you'll keep her in line."

"I'm sure I'll be able to do that with one leg," I said sarcastically.

"Right," said Darlene. Darlene never gets sarcasm.

I felt a little scared as I opened the door. My friends were all excited that I was coming back. I didn't know what I would do with myself. It wasn't going to be easy.

Lauren opened the door for me. One of the hardest things about being on crutches was never being able to open a door for myself.

I had only been away for a week, but it seemed like months. The gym was busy. The little kids were bouncing on the trampoline with Jodi's mom in charge.

Becky was working out on the uneven bars with Patrick spotting her.

"Cindi! Cindi!" Ti An's voice was high and squeaky. She ran up to me as if she wanted to throw her arms around me, but it's hard to throw your arms around someone using crutches. She stopped awkwardly and jumped on her tiptoes.

I grinned at her. I was surprised at how happy

I was to see her. She's such a pipsqueak. "Hi, Ti An. Last time I saw you I had two legs." I tapped my cast with my crutch.

Ti An looked horrified. "Your leg's still there, isn't it?" she asked.

I forgot she was just eight years old. "Ti An, it's just broken. It's in there."

"Was it in two pieces?" she asked. "I mean, did it go in different directions?"

"Ti An!" exclaimed Lauren, sounding annoyed. "Don't make Cindi talk about it."

"It's okay," I said. I liked Ti An asking direct questions. All the other Pinecones were so worried about my feelings that they hardly asked me about my leg.

"No, it wasn't in two pieces," I explained. "But I heard this crack and I knew it was broken."

"Far out," said Ti An. She sounded impressed.

"Then this ski patrol guy kept telling me that it wasn't broken. But I knew."

"Cindi, you don't have to talk about it if you don't want to," said Lauren.

"How did they get you down the mountain? Did you fly?" asked Ti An.

I laughed. I had visions of that horrible sled turning into a private jet and whizzing me in comfort down the mountain.

"What did I say that was so funny?" asked Ti An.

"She didn't fly down the mountain. She had to be taken down in a sled, and it was awful," said Darlene.

"I'm sorry," said Ti An. "I thought maybe they took you down in a helicopter." She looked down at my toes sticking out of my cast. My sock had fallen off and my toes were dirty.

"It's okay, Ti An," I said.

"Cindi! What are you doing here?" asked Ashley. Ashley was dressed in a red, white, and blue leotard. She had red hair bands holding her pigtails.

"I'm back," I said, smiling to myself. Ashley didn't like me any more than I liked her.

"But what can you do with a broken leg? I mean, won't you feel bad watching the rest of us work out?"

Darlene snorted. "That's very tactful of you, Ashley," she said.

"I was only thinking of Cindi," Ashley protested.

I grinned. "Sure, Ashley," I said. Actually, it felt much better to be back than I had expected.

Patrick came over to me, a big smile on his face. "Cindi, I've got the dumbbells all ready for you. And I want to see you on the bike."

Patrick took me over to the stationary bicycle that he normally keeps in the parents' lounge to give our moms and dads some exercise while they watch us.

"I brought it out into the gym," said Patrick. "I thought it would be more fun for you to be right in the middle of the action."

"How am I going to do this with one foot?" I asked. But Patrick helped me onto the bike. It was very high tech with a speedometer and even a mounted book rest in case you wanted to read while you biked. I was able to rest my cast on a metal bar sticking out from the bike. I found it was relatively easy to peddle with my good leg.

"This'll keep up your aerobic conditioning," said Patrick, "and the weights will keep you strong."

Becky stood a little bit behind Patrick. At first I thought she was embarrassed to see me since it was the first time since the accident. But she had her hands on her hips and a pout on her face. I realized she was just annoyed that I was getting so much attention.

"When I was in a cast you didn't tell me about the bike," Becky whined.

"I didn't have it then," said Patrick. Then he stared at my cast. "What is this?" he asked. "Nobody's written on it. We've got to do something about that!"

I blushed. "Uh . . . no," I stammered.

"Well, it happens that I'm a very good artist," said Patrick. "Come on. Get off the bike for a minute and sit down here. I know exactly what I want to do. Lauren, run into my office and in my top drawer you'll find a set of felt pens."

Patrick guided me to a chair. Suddenly I liked the idea of having a decorated cast. I don't know why I had been such a stick-in-the-mud about it before. My leg didn't hurt now, and I didn't feel so fragile.

Everybody gathered around as Lauren handed Patrick the pens. He drew the outline of an evergreen tree, the symbol of our gym. Then he filled it in with a green marker.

"It's really beautiful," I said.

"Wait," said Patrick. "I haven't finished." He took a brown pen and drew a pinecone on top of the evergreen. Then he drew little crutches underneath the pinecone.

Everybody laughed, including me. He labeled the pinecone "Cindi." Then he wrote, "I can't wait to get Cindi back on the beam." He signed it with a flourish, "Patrick."

"Now me," said Lauren. Patrick handed her the pen. Lauren thought for a moment. She drew a big heart. "I love you! Get well!" she wrote.

I felt silly, but it almost made me cry. Lauren and I have been friends for so long.

Soon my cast was filled up with drawings and signatures. Jodi is a great artist. She drew a cartoon of herself waving to me, and me sliding toward her flat on my back. Ti An drew me a flower.

Darlene tried to draw me swinging on the uneven bars in a cast, but I looked more like a monkey. I didn't care. I told her that her drawing was great.

Even Becky signed it. She wrote "Get well! Becky," in very neat block letters. "Sorry about your accident," she muttered.

I wondered if Becky felt guilty. I didn't have to wonder long. "Patrick," she complained, "how much time are we going to spend doing this? We're paying for gymnastics, you know."

"Becky," said Patrick sharply, "learning to care for your teammates is one of the most important lessons you can learn in gymnastics."

"I'm sorry," said Becky. She actually blushed.

"Besides," continued Patrick, "Cindi is still very much a valuable member of the team. She's not here just to work out on weights and the bicycle. Cindi, I want you to help me keep track of what everybody is doing. I'm going to put you in charge of the workout sheets."

I was used to seeing Patrick walking around with a clipboard, but I had never paid much attention to what he was doing with it. Patrick handed me a clipboard with a sheet for each girl and a list of strength and conditioning exercises in one column and another column for our routines on floor, beam, vault, and bars.

"You can be my second pair of eyes," said Patrick. "You can even do it from the bicycle." Patrick attached the clipboard to the book rest on the bicycle.

I looked up and grinned wickedly at my teammates, the Pinecones. "Okay, gang," I said. I glanced down at my clipboard. "Let's see forty stomach crunches."

All the Pinecones groaned in unison.

This wasn't going to be so bad after all. I loved being back in the gym, and I have to admit I didn't mind being in charge. In fact, I kind of liked it.

9

Everybody Hates Me! I Guess I'll Go Eat Worms

I had settled into a routine. Four times a week I came to the gym. I spent the first half hour doing some weights. Then I attached the clipboard to the bicycle, hiked up my cast, and pedaled while the Pinecones worked on new routines. Everyday I'd mark down how close each of them had come to completing the routine correctly.

Ti An was the first one to nail the new routine on the beam. Ti An always did what I asked her to, and even Ashley wasn't too bad, but my best friends were the ones who gave me the most trouble. Helping Patrick had made me see things in a totally new light.

I hadn't realized how much we Pinecones goofed off until I started keeping Patrick's records. My very best friends were among the worst goof-offs, especially Jodi. I used to find Jodi funny. I knew she was a flake, but it never bothered me.

I was watching Lauren up on the uneven bars. She looked sloppy, "Lauren, point your toes!" I yelled from the bicycle. She finished her dismount.

I told her that her feet were all wrong.

"Thanks," she grunted, but she gave me a dirty look.

"Next," I shouted. Jodi and Darlene were whispering together. "Jodi," I said impatiently. "It's your turn."

"Hold your horses," said Jodi as she chalked up. She walked over to where I was sitting on the bicycle and clapped her hands near my face, getting chalk dust on my nose.

"Why did you do that?" I complained.

"To lighten you up," said Jodi. "You need it."

"Yeah," said Lauren. "You're getting a little bossy. Ever since Patrick put that clipboard in your hand, you're taking yourself mighty seriously."

"I am not," I protested. My feelings were hurt.

Jodi went back to the chalk bin for a second

time. Gymnasts always use the chalk up as an excuse to waste time. I knew that Jodi needed to be pushed to do her best work.

"Come on, Jodi. You don't need more chalk." I clicked my ballpoint pen impatiently.

Jodi clapped her hands together to get rid of the loose chalk. She gave me a dirty look.

"What do I have to do?" she asked.

"A kip to the low bar, and then ten casts from the high bar." A cast is like a push-up done on the uneven bars. Nobody likes to practice them. They're exhausting.

"Ten!" exclaimed Jodi. "Get real."

I looked down at the clipboard. "This *is* real. That's what Patrick's got written down here for you."

"Well, I don't want to do ten," said Jodi. She grabbed hold of the low bar and pulled herself up. She swung up to the high bar.

She grinned down at me. I couldn't control her when she was ten feet over my head. Jodi did just three casts and then she circled back down to the low bar, and swung freely. She was teasing me.

"Jodi," I complained, "get back up and do seven more casts."

"You're the expert on casts," she said. "I can't

wait till you get yours off and we get that clipboard out of your hands."

"Are you going to do what I say?"

"I don't think so," said Jodi. She jumped down, grinning at me.

Patrick came up behind me. Jodi looked a little sheepish. "Hi, Patrick," she said.

"How's it going?" he asked.

"I've got seven more casts to do," said Jodi. She walked around and got back on the bars. She finished her seven casts. I marked them down on my clipboard, but my face was red.

Jodi would do them for Patrick, but she wouldn't do them for me. I tried to keep my temper. I didn't want to be a tattletale, but it made me mad.

None of the Pinecones was taking me seriously.

I got off the bike. My leg was itching terribly. I wanted to take a coat hanger and stick it underneath the cast. But I remembered that Dr. Heilbrun had warned me against doing that. I rubbed my leg near the top of my cast.

Becky saw me doing that. "How much longer?" she asked.

"I get it off in a week," I said.

"Your leg will be disgusting," she said. "I only

had a cast on for three weeks, and when it came off I thought my calf had withered away. It was this yukky pasty color, and I had grown long hairs. It looked like something from Frankenstein."

"Thanks, Becky, for cheering me up."

"I was just warning you," she said. Becky went off to the locker room.

The Pinecones finished their workout. Patrick came up to me. He was carrying my clipboard.

"Hey, coach, you left this on your bike," he said. He sat down next to me.

I took the clipboard.

"Why the long face, Cindi?" he asked me. "Are you getting anxious to get your cast off?"

"No . . . I mean yes," I stammered.

"You've been a real help to me," said Patrick.

"I haven't really," I said. "The Pinecones only really work when you're around," I said. "When it's just me, they fool around."

Patrick frowned. "Come on, Cindi. I seem to remember some times when you've fooled around, too."

I blushed. It was true that I did goof off sometimes. Patrick looked down at my cast.

"How are the muscles coming? Let me see?"

I cocked my arm to make my bicep bulge. Patrick pressed down, but my muscle was hard. He smiled at me. "I do believe you're going to come back stronger than ever," he said.

"Do you think so?" I asked.

"Absolutely," said Patrick. He looked across the floor where Lauren was working on her tumbling. "Lauren," he shouted. "Point your toes."

On her next roundoff, Lauren's toes were perfectly pointed. Patrick got up.

"The Pinecones workout is finished," said Patrick. "I'll see you tomorrow."

I grabbed for my crutches and hauled myself off the bench. I had left my knapsack next to the bike. I got it and pushed through the swinging door of the locker room. Then I stopped. I heard Lauren's voice, sounding unmistakably angry.

"Well, *I'm* her best friend. I should be the one to do it," she said.

"We're all in this together," said Jodi. "I don't think you should have to do it alone."

"Cindi'll be suspicious if you make it too obvious," said Darlene.

What was I going to be suspicious about? I knew that it was wrong to eavesdrop, but I couldn't make myself move. I let the door to the locker room close a little bit so that they wouldn't know I was listening.

"Personally," said Lauren, "I can't wait until it's all over."

Now I was sure I knew what they were talking about. My friends were sick of me bossing them around.

"Why don't we just talk to Patrick about it?" said Darlene. "That's the easiest thing to do. He can take charge."

"But we can't all go to Patrick. Cindi never leaves us alone. She's watching us all the time," complained Jodi. "I know Cindi. She's smart. She'll figure out what we're up to."

"Well, Lauren has been her friend for the longest time," admitted Darlene. "I guess it should be her."

"I agree," said Jodi. "And if we wait too long, it'll never work."

I bit my lip. Had I really gotten so bossy that my friends wanted to complain to Patrick?

What else could it be? It wasn't bad enough that I had a broken leg and couldn't do gymnastics, but now my friends were mad at me. They were going to take their complaints to Patrick, and then I'd be in hot water. I couldn't believe my own teammates were turning against me. I remembered the old song, "Everybody hates me. I guess I'll go eat worms." I used to laugh at that song. It wasn't funny anymore.

10

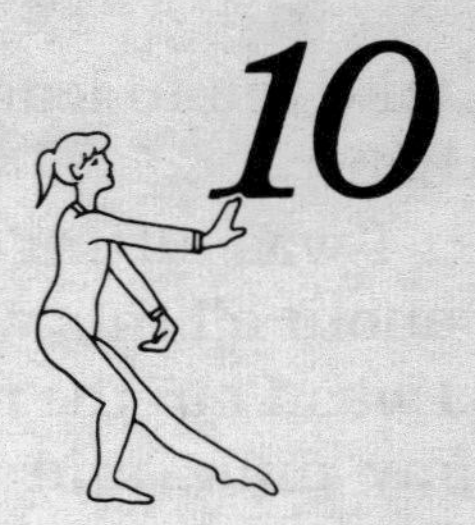

Don't Forget Your Cast!

Finally I was getting my cast off. I couldn't believe the day was actually here. After school, Mom was picking me up and we were going straight to Dr. Heilbrun's office. I couldn't wait. I was tired of wearing skirts. I was so sick of lugging my cast around, sticking it in a garbage bag in order to take a shower, feeling it every time I tried to turn in my sleep. I wouldn't miss it.

The last week seemed to take forever. I was bored with my routine at the gym. I never found out if Lauren had talked to Patrick. Patrick hadn't said anything to me.

Once my cast was off, I'd have to work hard to try to catch up. I had no idea how long it would take me to learn the new routines. I'd fallen far behind.

I was sitting in the school cafeteria, thinking about all this when Lauren sat down next to me. I wasn't in the mood to talk to her. I had forgotten my milk, and I reached for my crutches to go back in line.

"I'll get it for you," said Lauren. She popped up before I could stop her.

I still was mad at Lauren for what I had overheard in the locker room. I couldn't tell her why I was mad at her, because then I would have to admit that I had been a creep and eavesdropped.

Lauren brought me back the half pint of milk. "This time tomorrow, you can be getting it yourself, right?" she asked.

I nodded. "My cast comes off this afternoon."

"I bet you can't wait," she said.

"I can't wait till people stop asking me if I can't wait till my cast comes off."

"What's wrong? Did you get up on the wrong leg this morning?" complained Lauren. "You're a grouch today. It's supposed to be a red-letter day."

I nodded as I sipped my milk through the straw. I did feel like a grouch.

"Can I come with you?" Lauren asked.

"Come with me where?" I asked.

"To the doctor, silly," said Lauren. "I want to see them take your cast off."

"You don't have to do that."

"I want to go," said Lauren.

"Why should you want to go?" I asked. "It's going to be creepy. They have to saw it off. It'll be like seeing a horror movie."

Lauren cringed. Lauren hates horror movies. During the scary parts, she puts her jacket over her head.

"My appointment's at three-thirty after school. Mom's picking me up. If you come with me, you'll have to miss gymnastics," I said.

"You'd go with me if I had a cast on my leg," Lauren argued. "Let me come. I can go to gymnastics every day."

"Yeah, but *I* won't be around to boss you this afternoon," I said meaningfully. Why did she want to come with me? I thought she was mad at me. I hated that Lauren had a secret from me. If she was mad at me, why didn't she just say so? Why did she have to go behind my back to Patrick?

I was confused. Had I heard it wrong? I distinctly heard the Pinecones say that Lauren was the one who was supposed to do it. Do what? It couldn't have been to go to the doctor with me.

Lauren wasn't really a very sneaky person. I

knew she couldn't keep a secret very well.

"Lauren, come on. I know," I said.

"Know what?" Lauren asked angrily.

"I know what you had to do, and now you're feeling guilty."

"I'm not feeling guilty," protested Lauren. But she was blushing.

I was the one feeling guilty. I didn't want to confess that I had eavesdropped. "I guess you can come to the doctor's with me, if you want," I said.

"Well, good," said Lauren. "Then it's settled. I'm coming."

I waited for Lauren to say something else, about how she had decided that our friendship was too important, that I was her best friend no matter what the other Pinecones said. But she didn't say another word.

After school, she carried my knapsack for me. "Just think," she said. "In a couple of hours, you'll have both hands free and be able to carry your own things again."

"I can't wait," I said, as my crutches dug into my armpits and I swung out to the parking lot.

Mom didn't seem very surprised that Lauren wanted to go with me.

We didn't have to wait long at Dr. Heilbrun's

office. Lauren took out her homework in the waiting room. "I'm not going in to watch any buzz saw," she said, as the nurse opened the door for me. "I'll stay out here, if that's okay."

"I don't blame you," I said. But I wondered why she had insisted on coming if she didn't want to see the big unveiling.

Dr. Heilbrun took me into an examining room. She helped me onto the table. "You've got some beautiful drawings on this cast," she said. "What's the evergreen for?"

"It's my gymnastics school," I said. "My coach, Patrick, drew that."

"I like the pinecone on crutches," said Dr. Heilbrun. "I bet you're glad to get this thing off," she said.

I nodded, but in a strange way, I wasn't half as excited as I thought I should be. In fact, I was scared.

Dr. Heilbrun lowered an X-ray machine. "Let me get some pictures of it first," she said. "We have to see if it set all right."

"What if it didn't?" I asked.

"Then we'd have to keep it in a cast," said Dr. Heilbrun. "Don't worry, Cindi. When I took pictures of it two weeks ago, I told you it was healing fine."

I worried.

Dr. Heilbrun took the X rays. She went away for a few minutes.

Dr. Heilbrun came back into the room. She was smiling. "It healed beautifully," she said. She put the X ray up on the wall and showed me the line of the break. "It's perfectly aligned," she said proudly, as if she had done it herself.

"Now, let's get that cast off." Dr. Heilbrun brought out a little machine with a round blade. "Do you really saw it off?" I asked.

"This saw cuts by vibration. It can't cut you."

She turned the machine on and put her hand right on the blade. She showed me her hand. There was no cut on it. "Give me your arm," she said. "I'll show you. You'll feel a tickling, strange sensation, but it can't cut you."

She put the blade on my forearm for a minute. It gave me the creeps, but it didn't cut into my arm.

I sat up and watched as she took the machine and made a straight line through the cast. Every time the blade came close to my skin, I wanted to jump. The saw was incredibly noisy. Mom held my hand. When Dr. Heilbrun turned off the saw, the cast had a fine line through it, but it wasn't off my leg.

She took a clamp and began to break it away.

"Wait," I shouted. "Can you save the part with the pinecone and the evergreen on it?"

"I'll try," said Dr. Heilbrun. The cast fell away. I looked down at my leg. My skin was yellow and icky. Flakes were peeling off as if I had gotten a ghostly sunburn. In fact my leg was even more disgusting than Becky had said.

Dr. Heilbrun took a cream and rubbed it on my leg. The cream soothed the itching.

I rubbed my leg. It was the first time I had touched it in so long.

I looked at my two legs side by side. I couldn't believe the difference. My right thigh was about half the size of my left. The calf on my broken leg looked withered, and my leg pointed to the side. I had to force my toes straight, but as soon as I relaxed, my leg pointed out again, like a dancer in constant third position.

"This is sick," I said to Dr. Heilbrun.

"The skin will heal quickly," she said. "We'll wrap your leg in an Ace bandage just to give you a little support."

"Can I walk on it?" I asked.

"It's very weak," she said. "You'll need the crutches for a couple of days, but you can start to put some weight on it."

Dr. Heilbrun helped me down from the table. "Let's see you walk down the corridor," she said.

"Piece of cake," I said. I took two steps, with my crutches, and my leg almost buckled under me. I looked back at the doctor.

"My leg's pointed in the wrong direction. Is it going to stay like this?"

"It's been immobile in that turned out position for a long time," said Dr. Heilbrun. "That's normal. It'll get straight very soon."

I tried to take a step. I felt seasick. I could only put a little weight on my heel. But I put one foot ahead of the other until I reached the end of the corridor.

"Now come back," said Dr. Heilbrun.

I headed back toward Dr. Heilbrun and my mom, but it wasn't easy.

Dr. Heilbrun studied me. "Your left leg is very strong," she said. "Usually both legs atrophy a little."

"I did a lot of pedaling on a bike with one leg," I explained.

"I'd like you to take it easy for the next week or so," said Dr. Heilbrun. "But after that, if you're feeling all right, I think you should be back up on the beam or doing cartwheels. You're still in very good shape."

"I don't feel like I'm in good shape," I said. "I feel like a wimp."

"It'll take you a while to get your balance back,"

said Dr. Heilbrun, "but you look good."

"I do?" I thought she was crazy. I had expected that when my cast came off that I'd feel normal again. Instead I felt almost half-naked without it, and I certainly couldn't walk normally. I was walking like a toddler.

Dr. Heilbrun patted me on the back. "As it heals the bone gets stronger. Your leg is actually stronger than it was before."

I wanted to tell Dr. Heilbrun that I didn't feel strong. My right leg looked like it didn't belong to me. It was more Ti An's size than mine.

I walked toward the waiting room. "Hold on a second," called Dr. Heilbrun. "You're forgetting something."

I turned around. Dr. Heilbrun was holding the two halves of my cast. "You don't want to forget these, do you?"

Maybe I did, I thought.

11

Cast-Off

Lauren studied my leg. "It's not half as yucky as I thought it would be."

"How much more yucky could it be?" I exclaimed.

We walked out to the car. "You walk funny, though," said Lauren. "I thought you'd be able to throw your crutches away, like in a movie."

"I can barely stand up, even with the crutches," I said. "I can't tell you how weird it feels," I said. "It feels like something is missing."

Lauren played with the two pieces of my cast "We could always glue it back together," she said.

"No way," I said.

"Let's stop at the gym and show everybody how you look," said Lauren.

I shook my head. "I'm not in the mood."

"Come on," said Lauren. "It's just for a minute."

I kept rubbing my calf.

"I told you, I don't feel like it," I said. "My leg stinks. I need a bath."

Lauren pouted. Mom glanced at me as if she thought I was being a spoilsport, but I really didn't want to go to the gym.

"Uh, I've got to go to the gym," said Lauren. "I left my watch there on Friday, and my mom will kill me if I don't pick it up. I promised her I'd pick it up."

"But if you promised her, how come you insisted on coming to the doctor's with me?" I argued. "You knew I wasn't going to gymnastics."

"Oh, come on, Cindi," said Mom. "We can just stop off there. It's right on the way. It'll only take a minute."

"Oh, all right," I said. I didn't want to get the reputation of being a total grouch.

We pulled up in front of the gym. There were a number of cars parked outside. I looked at my watch. It was almost five o'clock. Practice would be nearly over.

"I'll wait for you in the car," I said to Lauren.

"Come on in," said Lauren.

I shook my head no.

Mom dug into her handbag. "Oh, my goodness!" she said. "I forgot I owe Patrick a check for your lessons. Cindi, will you take this in for me?"

"You can give it to him yourself," I said. "I'll wait here."

Mom and Lauren looked at each other. I knew I was being a pain in the neck, but I couldn't help myself. Mom sounded annoyed. "It'll save time if you do it. I want to run over to the mall and pick up some groceries. I'll meet you girls back here in a few minutes."

I took the check from Mom and opened the car door. "Well, all right," I said grudgingly.

We walked into the gym. "CINDI, THIS WILL JUST TAKE A MINUTE," shouted Lauren.

"Why are you shouting?" I asked. "I can hear you."

"CINDI, WAS I SHOUTING?" yelled Lauren.

I wondered if something was going wrong with Lauren's hearing.

I opened the door to the gym.

All the Pinecones were poised at the edge of a mat. Patrick stood to the side.

"On your mark, get set, go!" he shouted. One

by one, the Pinecones did a cartwheel down a line until they jumped up right in front of me, yelling, "SURPRISE!"

I couldn't figure out what was going on. Then I looked up. Strung across the gym was a huge banner. CAST PARTY FOR CINDI!

"What . . . ?" I could feel myself blushing.

"It's a cast-off party," said Lauren, giving me a hug.

"I don't believe you guys," I said.

Patrick put his arm around me. "The Pinecones have been planning this party for the past week," he said. "We've got ice cream and cake."

I stared at Lauren. "All that stuff about your watch . . . and Mom giving me the check."

Lauren giggled. "I thought we were going to have to drag you out of the car."

"So, how's the leg?" Jodi asked. "Is it there?" she nudged Ti An.

"The doctor says it's okay," I said. "But it looks weird."

"Let me see! Let me see!" shouted Ti An. I couldn't resist her. I remembered when I was eight I needed to see every bruise my brothers got at football games.

I rolled down my knee sock. My calf muscle looked tiny.

"Oh, yuk!" said Ashley, pinching her nose. "It's all gooey."

"That's just some cream the doctor put on," I said. I was embarrassed. "I should have gone home and taken a bath. It'll be the first bath without having to put my leg in a garbage bag."

"We wanted to celebrate right away," said Lauren. "You can take a bath anytime."

"I'm just glad we can get that clipboard out of your hands," joked Jodi. "Now you'll be just another gymnast."

Patrick smiled at me. "Cindi will never be just another gymnast," he said.

"Come on," said Lauren, who's always interested in food. "Let's stop the chitchat and get to the cake."

Patrick led me into the parents' lounge. Mom was waiting for us there.

"You knew, didn't you?" I said to her.

She grinned to me. "If you made one more excuse to wait in the car, I was going to hit you over the head and carry you in unconscious."

"Well, I guess I was in a grumpy mood," I admitted.

"With friends like yours, you can't stay grouchy very long," said Mom. "Go on, enjoy your party."

All the gymnasts were lined up next to the table, waiting for me. They all looked so happy. Now I knew what they had been talking about in the locker room. I felt like such a jerk to have suspected that they hated me.

"Cut the cake! Cut the cake!" yelled Lauren.

I walked to the table.

The cake was in the shape of a broken leg with white frosting and an evergreen in the middle.

"The lady at the bakery thought I was crazy when I ordered a cake in the shape of a broken leg," said Patrick. "She thought it was a sick joke."

"Look!" Darlene pointed to two figures on the cake. One was a skier, the other a gymnast. Darlene hugged me. "That's you, now that you're well again."

"I don't feel one hundred percent, yet," I said.

"You will," said Patrick, "you will. You'll be back to normal soon."

"Yeah, you've got to learn the new routine, and then we can have our pasta party, right Patrick?" said Lauren.

"Lauren, you have a few tricks to clean up, too," said Patrick. "But you're right. As soon as Cindi nails the new routines, I owe the Pinecones a pasta party. I have a feeling we won't have to wait long."

I wished I felt as confident as he did.

I didn't.

But I ate my cake and I didn't complain. What did I have to complain about? My cast was off. My friends were throwing me a party. Only an idiot would stay in a bad mood. I wasn't an idiot.

12

Who Needs Pity?

I've got to admit that human bodies are pretty amazing. I hadn't done anything, and my body had healed itself. I mean, if you cut a piece of paper with scissors, then patch it with Scotch tape, and you leave it like that for a year, the paper won't grow back together.

I had seen the pictures of the bone in my leg. It was like a torn piece of paper, but the two ends had grown back together and they didn't have to use glue or Scotch tape or anything.

The more I exercised the stronger I got. Patrick gave me a whole new series of strengthening exercises. He made me listen to the music for our floor exercise while I was bicycling, and I started to work out on the beam and the bars and the vault. At first I was very tentative, but soon I got some of my old skills back.

By the end of a couple weeks, Dr. Heilbrun said that there was nothing I couldn't do that I had done before.

Now my body was okay. It was my mind that was a mess.

I first noticed it when I was working on the uneven bars. Patrick wanted me to do a jump to a back hip circle on the high bar. It was a move I had done hundreds of times before my accident and it was part of a new routine. I stood on the lower bar with my hands on the upper bar. All I had to do was to cast off high enough so that I could get around backwards on the high bar. Patrick was underneath me if I fell.

I licked my lips and did a hesitant little jump on the low bar.

"Do you call that a jump?" Patrick asked. "That won't give you enough lift. Push off!"

"I can't," I said.

"Cindi, I'm right here," said Patrick patiently. "Of course you can do it."

I shook my head.

"Cindi, 'can't' isn't a word that I hear from you."

"I can't do it, Patrick," I said.

I think Patrick thought I was joking. It was such a simple move.

"I'll hold you," said Patrick.

"No."

I looked around the gym. The mats seemed so far below me. The high bar had never seemed so high before.

"Do it!" said Patrick.

I couldn't. I totally lost it. I jumped down from the bars. I ran from the gym. Lauren gave me a stricken look. I ran into the locker room. It's the one place that Patrick couldn't follow me.

I locked myself into one of the bathroom stalls. I didn't want anybody to see me. I felt like such a fool. It was such an easy move. I had just frozen up there. I had been scared before. When Patrick was teaching me the Eagle, I had been really afraid, and it took everything I had to keep going.

But this fear was so different. This fear just froze me solid.

I wiped my eyes. I wasn't a coward. I knew that. I went back out to the gym.

"Patrick, I'm sorry," I said. He was spotting Becky on the uneven bars. She whipped through her routine as if it were nothing.

Patrick didn't take his eyes off Becky. It was so stupid of me to be afraid. Patrick was one of the strongest spotters and coaches I had ever had. He was watching Becky every second to make sure she wasn't in trouble. If she started to slip, Patrick would be there in a split second.

Becky finished her routine. "That was terrific," said Patrick. "You need just a little more amplitude on your dismount, but otherwise it was great."

Becky was breathing hard from the exertion. She bent over with her hands on her knees to catch her breath. I had to admit that while I might not like Becky, she worked hard. If I ever wanted to catch up to her, I'd have to work hard, too. I couldn't wait to get back on the bars and try again.

"Okay, Cindi," said Patrick. "Ready?" I studied Patrick's face to see if he was mad at me for running away.

He didn't seem to be. I did my mount onto the lower bar. I pointed my toes and it went fine. I was feeling good.

Then I got in position for my jump to the high bar. I put my feet on the low bar and grabbed the high bar.

Before I could push off, it happened again. I just froze. I couldn't believe it! Patrick stretched his right arm out toward the high bar. He could almost touch it, and I knew that as I circled the bar, he could catch me and push me around.

But I couldn't move.

I looked down at him. Patrick didn't say anything. He was waiting for me.

"Take it slow," he said finally. "I'll work you around."

"It's so easy," I whispered.

"It's been a while," said Patrick. "Just push off. I'll do most of the work."

I knew in my head that there was no danger that Patrick would let me fall. But my head wasn't connected to my body. Dr. Heilbrun had said that my leg was stronger than ever before, but those were just words. What if I broke it again with just one little slip?

"Patrick, I can't do it," I said.

"Hop down," said Patrick. "You're just coming back from the injury. We don't have to push it."

Becky was looking up at me. I actually thought I saw pity in her eyes. The last thing in the world that I wanted was pity from Becky.

I didn't want anybody's pity. But what if I really had lost it? This didn't feel like fear. I had felt fear before. But always it was something that came and went. This felt like something solid that would never go away.

13

All Alone

I didn't quit, but I wasn't the same gymnast that I was before. I went to class, but I felt like I was going through the motions.

About a week later, I was watching Ti An up on the beam. She was doing the new routine without any mistakes. Patrick wasn't pushing me. And none of the Pinecones were riding me. Everyone was being a little bit too nice. Nobody talked about the pasta party. I knew we weren't having it because of me, but it was never mentioned. It was as if the Pinecones and Patrick were treating me with kid gloves. I didn't like it.

Jodi was next in line. I stood behind her. Jodi was biting her fingernails. Ti An did a perfect

Valdez to back walkover. She almost floated up from her sitting position on the beam into the back walkover. It looked beautiful.

"I wish I were three feet tall like Ti An," said Jodi. "Maybe then I'd get around as fast."

"Don't be jealous," I teased. When Ti An had first joined our team we had all been jealous because she was good and so tiny and cute.

Ti An skipped over to us. "You looked great," I said.

"Thanks," said Ti An. "Good luck, Jodi."

Jodi just grunted. She got up on the beam. "Try the Valdez back-walkover," said Patrick.

"I *knew* you'd say that," said Jodi, half-joking.

"It's the one new element in the routine that's shaky for you," said Patrick.

Patrick got in position to spot Jodi through the move. Jodi lost her balance and wobbled. She fell off the beam onto the mat. She started laughing nervously.

Patrick wasn't smiling. "Up and try it again," he said.

"Aren't there laws against this?" asked Jodi as she mounted the beam and tried it again.

She fell off a second time. This time she didn't laugh.

"Come on, one more time," said Patrick. "You had it last week." This time Patrick held onto

Jodi and made sure that she didn't fall off the beam.

"Okay," said Patrick. "Do it yourself."

Jodi concentrated. She almost lost her balance on the back-walkover, but she held on and she finished the routine.

"Whew," said Jodi when she returned to the line. "That wasn't easy."

"You almost got it perfect," said Ti An.

Jodi gave her a dirty look. "Almost doesn't count. You're the one who can do that move perfectly."

"Don't worry, Ti An," I said. "We're all just green with envy that you can do it."

"Yeah," said Lauren. "We're 'ever green' envy monsters, Ti An. We 'pine cone' we can't do what you do."

I groaned. "That's the worst pun I've ever heard."

"I don't want you to be green," said Ti An so seriously that she made me laugh.

"Excuse me," said Patrick. "Are the Pinecones comedians or gymnasts?"

"Why not both?" I asked.

Patrick laughed. "Come on, Cindi. It's your turn. Let me see your Valdez back-walkover. Once you've nailed that the rest of the routine is easy."

"Go for it, Cindi," said Lauren. "You can waltz right through it. And finally we can get our pasta."

"Yeah," said Ti An. "What exactly is pasta?"

"You're stupid, Ti An," said Ashley.

"Don't call Ti An stupid," I said. "Pasta's just noodles, and Ti An uses her noodle all the time."

I took a step toward the beam. I felt very loose. I mounted the beam.

I got into position for the Valdez. I extended my right leg, so I could push off with my left leg.

I started to push myself backwards, and I stopped. My arms were shaking.

"Let me do it on the low beam," I muttered.

"Okay," said Patrick.

Quickly I got into the correct position on the low beam. I did the move with no problem. Patrick watched me.

He patted the high beam. "Get back up here," he said. "You're ready."

I nodded, but my heart was beating overtime as if I were working hard. But I wasn't. It was an easy move.

I climbed back up on the high beam. I was sweating now. The beam didn't feel right. Even before I got into position, I knew I wasn't going to be able to do it.

"I don't feel well," I said to Patrick. "I need a drink of water."

"Go get one," said Patrick. He nodded to me as I got off the beam. Patrick was going easy on me.

I went to the water fountain. I couldn't remember ever sweating so much.

Becky was there in front of me. I felt like I was dying of thirst.

"Hurry, please," I urged her.

"Hold your horses," said Becky. She straightened up and looked me in the face.

"You look awful," she said.

I bent down and took a sip of water. "You sick?" Becky asked.

I shook my head no. "I'm okay. I'm just having one of those days."

I went to a bench to sit down. Maybe I was coming down with the flu. I almost hoped that I was getting sick. But what if I wasn't? I looked down at my right leg. I was probably the only one who who could see that it was still smaller than my left. But not by much.

I wanted to cry. But I'm not a crybaby.

Patrick didn't call me back to the beam. I looked at my watch. Our session was almost over. The other Pinecones finished up and went into the locker room. I followed them.

"Get your shoes out of here," said Lauren angrily.

"I didn't know it was *your* leotard," said Ashley.

Lauren was having a stupid argument with Ashley because Ashley had put her gym shoes on top of Lauren's leotard. Just a typical scene with the Pinecones. It all seemed so silly and boring.

I started to change into my jeans and sweatshirt. "Hey, Cindi," shouted Darlene. "Want to come over to my house? My dad got me a video of the Olympics. We can watch the Americans get cheated out of the bronze one more time."

"No, thanks," I said. I wasn't in the mood for any more gymnastics.

"Come on," urged Darlene. "It'll be a gas."

"Cindi's been acting like she's out of gas," said Ashley, as she grabbed her gym shoes from Lauren.

"What does that mean?" asked Lauren angrily.

I knew what Ashley meant. If it weren't for me, every Pinecone would be doing the new routine. If it weren't for me, they would have had their pasta party long ago. "I was just making a joke," whined Ashley. She looked up at me. "It must take a long time to come back from a broken leg. You're sure not the same gymnast you were before."

"You shut up," snapped Jodi. "You can't talk to Cindi like that."

"Jodi," I said, "Ashley's right. I'm not any good anymore."

"Huh?" Jodi looked as if I had just slapped her across the face.

"You know," said Becky, "it's a proven fact that some gymnasts never come back from an accident. I'm not saying that'll happen to you, Cindi, but it happens."

"Why, you . . ." sputtered Lauren. Lauren is the one who *always* says "It's a proven fact." She knew Becky was mocking her. Lauren leapt across the bench and shoved Becky against the wall. Lauren is about half Becky's size, but she caught Becky so much by surprise that Becky couldn't do anything.

Lauren was ready to punch Becky out.

"Lauren!" I screamed. I grabbed Lauren from the back and pulled her off Becky. Patrick might throw Lauren out of the club for fighting.

I held Lauren's arms. "Becky can't talk to you like that," yelled Lauren. "She can't talk to any Pinecone like that."

Becky was dusting off her leotard. "Becky may be right," I said. "Maybe I have lost it. Maybe it's time for me to quit."

Nobody said a word for a while after that. I

finished packing up my gym bag. I started to leave.

Suddenly Darlene grabbed my forearm. “You’re coming to my house,” she said quietly.

“Darlene, I’m not in the mood,” I said.

Darlene almost never gets angry, but she looked angry right then. “You’re tearing us apart,” she said.

“I’m sorry,” I muttered. “There’s nothing I can do about it.” Then I left. I felt all alone.

14

Tears

I went home by myself, but I couldn't get Darlene's words out of my mind. She said I was tearing the Pinecones apart, but I was the one who was being torn apart. There were two things I had always been sure of — that I loved gymnastics and that it was something I could do. Now I wasn't sure of anything.

Jared was sitting in the kitchen with his homework spread out all over the table. Tim was helping him with his math.

I got myself a glass of milk. "What's for dinner?" I asked.

"Pizza," said Tim. "Dad's on a flight and Mom's got a meeting. It's just us."

I almost started to cry. Tim stared at me. "What's wrong with pizza?" he asked.

I wiped my nose with my sleeve. "Nothing!" I shouted.

"Cindi, are you okay?" Tim asked.

I felt lousy. "No," I admitted.

"Can we help?" Tim asked. Jared looked up at me. Even he would have helped if he could, but I couldn't think of anything that *anyone* could do.

"What's wrong?" Jared asked.

"I don't know," I said. Suddenly I knew that I had to be with the Pinecones. "Can you drive me over to Darlene's?" I sniffed.

"Did you Pinecones have a fight?" Jared asked. Jared always loved gossip.

"Shut up, Jared," said Tim. I was grateful to him. "Sure, Cindi, I'll drive you," he said.

Sometimes Tim is the best older brother in the world. He didn't ask me any stupid questions. He just put on his jacket and drove me over to Darlene's. I sat huddled in the corner of the front seat. It was dark out, and my mood felt as black as the woods outside the range of our headlights.

Tim pulled up in front of the gates at Darlene's house. "Do you want to call me when you're ready to come home?" he asked.

"Thanks, Tim," I said.

Tim patted me on the shoulder. "You've had a lousy couple of months, haven't you?" he said. "Breaking your leg and all."

"It's been the pits," I admitted.

"Does Darlene know you're coming over?" Tim asked.

I shook my head no. "She asked me before, but I didn't want to go. I'm having an awful time at gymnastics. I think I want to quit."

Tim wasn't shocked. "Don't make that decision about quitting when you're in a rotten mood," he said, finally.

"When am I not in a rotten mood?" I asked. "I should just quit and get it over with."

"The Pinecones wouldn't be the same without you."

"They'd be better off," I said. "They'd all be eating pasta by now if it weren't for me."

"Huh?" said Tim.

"Never mind," I said. "I've just lost it. It makes no sense to do gymnastics if you're afraid all the time."

"Don't do anything too hasty," said Tim.

I went up and rang the doorbell. Darlene's mom opened it. "Hi, Cindi," she said. "I was wondering where you were. All the other Pinecones are here, even little Ti An. You look terrific. How's your leg? Is it hurting you?"

"Not really," I said.

"Everyone's down in the basement watching the videotape," she said. "Why don't you go down and join them?"

I waved to Tim who was still sitting outside in the car. Then I sighed.

I walked toward Darlene's basement. Music was playing on the TV and nobody heard me go down the stairs.

I just stood at the entrance.

Finally Darlene looked up. She pushed a button on the remote control and the TV stopped.

I tried to smile, but I couldn't. Lauren and Jodi looked up, too.

Lauren shoved over on the couch to make room for me between her and Ti An.

Darlene stared at me. "Cindi, are you okay?" she asked.

"I'm okay," I muttered. "I'm sorry for the way I acted back at the gym. I know you guys were just trying to defend me. Forget about it."

"We can't," said Jodi. "We were talking about you. We're worried. You don't seem yourself."

"I thought you were watching the video," I said.

"Nobody was in the mood," said Lauren. "We *were* all talking about you. We were going to call you up. I'm so glad you're here."

I shrugged. "I don't know. I wasn't coming. I went home, but it didn't feel right, so I got Tim to bring me here. But . . ." I paused. I wanted to say I was quitting, but I couldn't get the words out. I just shrugged again. "Don't make a big deal out of me, okay?"

"Stop saying 'okay,' " said Darlene. "It drives me crazy."

"Okay," I said, trying to make a joke, but Darlene wasn't having any jokes.

"You haven't really been okay since you broke your leg," said Darlene.

I took a deep breath.

"I know," I said.

Then the strangest feeling came over me. I began to cry. I started crying so hard that it scared me. I didn't even know why I was crying.

Lauren put her arms around me. I tried to stop, but I couldn't.

"I'm sorry . . . I'm sorry," I blubbered. All the Pinecones were hugging me. We must have looked ridiculous.

I hiked my T-shirt out of the waistband of my jeans and used the bottom of it to wipe my tears.

"I don't know why I did that," I said. I looked at my friends. They were all crying, too. "Why are you crying?" I asked.

"Just because," said Darlene. Then she started

to half cry and laugh at the same time.

"Cut it out," I cried, but the tears kept coming. Finally I took a big sniff. I was embarrassed.

"You know, that's the first time I ever saw you cry," said Lauren. "And I've known you a long time."

"I feel like an idiot," I sniffed.

"You didn't even cry when you broke your leg," said Darlene.

"I was trying to be brave," I said.

Darlene looked at me. "We all cried when you broke your leg," she said. "What does that make us? Cowards?"

"No, of course not," I said, trying to smile.

Lauren brought out a big box of tissues. "Maybe we should change our names to Weeping Willows," she said as she passed the box around.

I started to laugh. It felt like the first real laugh I had had in a long time.

Lauren put the box back down. "Okay," she said. "Now you've got to promise us one thing."

"What's that?" I asked.

"No more talk about quitting, right?"

I took another tissue.

"I can't promise that," I said softly.

My friends looked as if they were all going to start crying again, but I was just being honest.

15

A Sense of Humor

The next day I got to the gym early. I waited for a minute when Patrick was alone. He was out on the floor adjusting the uneven bars. I helped him secure the wires.

"You check these every day, don't you?" I said.

"More than once a day," said Patrick. "I don't want any unnecessary accidents."

"What's a necessary accident?" I asked.

"Touché," said Patrick. "What's on your mind, Cindi? Is the accident still bothering you?"

"My leg feels fine," I said.

"That's not what I asked," said Patrick. Nobody would ever accuse Patrick of being dumb. "Cindi, why are you here early? Did you want to talk?"

I nodded. "Some people say that you never come back after an accident."

Patrick raised his eyebrows. "Some people?" he asked. "Who's been filling your head with that kind of negative garbage?"

I didn't answer.

Patrick sighed. "Never mind. I can guess." Patrick walked over to the floor mats and checked to see that they were all aligned.

I followed him. "Well, isn't it true sometimes?" I asked. "Maybe after an accident some people are just never the same."

Patrick steered me over to a bench on the side of the gym. "Cindi, you're the same person you were before you broke your leg."

"I don't think so," I said quietly. "You don't know what happened to me yesterday. I was over at Darlene's, with the other Pinecones. Suddenly I started bawling like a baby. Real gymnasts don't break down and cry. I never used to do that."

"A broken leg's tough. I've been expecting you to break down here," said Patrick. "What did the Pinecones do when you started crying?"

I gave a half-laugh. "They started crying, too."

"So does that mean they're not real gymnasts?" Patrick asked.

"No," I admitted.

"Cindi, what did you do when your accident happened?"

"I could hear it snap," I whispered.

Patrick nodded.

"And the first ski patrol man didn't believe me. I *knew* it was broken. But I didn't cry."

"Why?" asked Patrick.

"I was too scared. I didn't want them to see me cry."

"But now that you're okay maybe you needed to cry. It must have been pretty scary," said Patrick. "No wonder you feel different."

"But I *am* different now. You've got to admit I'm not even doing easy tricks anymore. I'll never get the new routine."

"Of course you're different," said Patrick. "Now you know you can get hurt. It's part of growing up. You will be different from kids who have never gotten hurt, but it doesn't mean that you have to quit."

"But I just can't do it anymore," I cried.

"Right," said Patrick. "Actually, I was expecting somebody superhuman to come back from a broken leg. Instead, you're still Cindi."

"What do you mean by that?" I asked suspiciously.

Patrick was smiling at me. "Sometimes, Cindi, you were afraid even before you broke your leg. So is everybody else. Think about it."

I looked out at the gym.

"Your accident changed you, but it doesn't have to be for the worse. It changed all your friends. They were all scared. In fact, I know Jodi still thinks it's her fault."

"It wasn't," I said. "All she did was wave to me. I was the one who slipped."

"But all Jodi remembers is that you looked up at her, and then you fell. She has to learn to live with it. You have to live with the fact that bones can break. It can be scary admitting you're vulnerable. Things aren't always in our control."

"I was sure out of control on the ski slope," I said.

"Nobody is one hundred percent in control," said Patrick. "Think about the other gymnasts you know. I always know when they're afraid. I bet you do, too."

I thought about it. Darlene always gives out these little hoots when she's afraid. Jodi pretends she's never scared, and then she bites her fingernails. Lauren makes jokes just to prove she's not afraid. Ti An gets quieter and quieter when she's frightened. Now that I thought about it, I realized that Ashley and Becky act like bullies just to cover up the fact that they're scared.

"What did you do when you were afraid before?" Patrick asked me.

"I just made myself do it," I admitted. "But what if I just can't do gymnastics anymore?"

Patrick didn't look as shocked as I expected. "Nobody can know that but you," he said. "But you're an athlete, Cindi. You're human, but you're an athlete."

"Now, what does that mean?" I asked.

Patrick patted me on the back. "Just think about it." He looked across the room as the Pinecones filed in. "Darlene!" he shouted. "Point your toes."

Darlene immediately pointed her toes.

I got up, feeling more confused than ever. Becky passed by me. "I hear you're thinking of quitting, huh?" she asked.

Rumors spread fast around our gym. Before I could answer her, Becky continued. "I'm not surprised," she said. "Not everyone can come back from an injury the way I did when I was hurt."

"Becky?" I asked. "Are you feeling guilty because of my accident?"

"Of course not," said Becky. "It wasn't my fault."

"Then what's your excuse for being such a grade-A turkey foot?" I asked.

Becky's mouth opened. "I'm not a turkey foot!" she exclaimed.

"Get real," I said.

"*You* get real," said Becky. "Who do you think you are?"

"I'm only human," I answered.

"I don't get it," exclaimed Becky as if I had asked her a riddle. Maybe I had.

I walked away from her. She was the last person I wanted to be around.

I thought about what Patrick had said. I loved hearing him say, "Cindi, you're an athlete." I couldn't give *that* up.

I went over to the beam, where the Pinecones were standing in line. We were starting out on the beam. I stood behind Lauren.

"What did you say to Becky?" she asked. "She looks like she's in shock."

"She thought I was a quitter," I said.

Lauren started to smile. "And what did you tell her?" Lauren asked.

"I'm only human," I answered.

Lauren looked puzzled.

"Cindi," said Patrick, "are you ready?" He patted the beam.

I nodded. "What do you want to do today?" Patrick asked.

I sighed. "I'll try the whole routine . . . with the Valdez back-walkover."

Patrick nodded approvingly. "Do you want to do it on the low beam first?" he asked. "It's your choice."

I shook my head no. "I want to do it on the high beam."

I sat down on the beam with my right leg bent. It had always been my stronger leg before. It was time to test it.

I took a deep breath and then swung my left leg into the air over my head and pushed backwards, arching my back into the walkover.

I completed the move.

Patrick was grinning up at me. I hopped down, and Patrick gave me a hug.

"What was so great about that?" Becky asked. "It's not such a hard move."

"It was for me," I said.

"Cindi," said Patrick, "you couldn't have made me prouder if you had won a gold medal in the Olympics."

"Patrick!" shouted Jodi. "I think you owe the Pinecones a pasta dinner."

Becky gave me a dirty look. "You get all the breaks," she said sourly.

I cracked up. The other Pinecones heard Becky and started to laugh. Patrick tried to stop himself, but he took one look at my face and started laughing, too.

"What's so funny?" insisted Becky. "I don't get it."

"That's the breaks," I said. "Some people have a sense of humor, some people don't."

16

Only Human

Patrick had a little kitchen built into the gym that none of us even knew about. It was in a tiny room outside of his office. There was the refrigerator that mostly held ice and soft drinks, and a hot plate. It was hard to imagine it as the gourmet center of a great meal, but Patrick outdid himself making us spaghetti sauce with sausage and onion. The whole gym was going to smell of garlic and onions, but the sauce he made was great.

It was so much fun to be in the gym in the evening and not have to do gymnastics. It was like a holiday.

"This is neat," said Lauren, as she went back

for a second helping. "I think we should make this a tradition."

"I think we should make it a weekly tradition," said Jodi.

"We'll see about that," said Patrick. He looked over at me. "Cindi, do you want seconds?"

I shook my head. I was stuffed.

"It was worth waiting for," said Darlene, going up and getting some more.

"I'm sorry everybody had to wait for me," I said.

Jodi threw a strand of spaghetti at me. "You turkey," she said. "We didn't mind."

"Turkey!" I exclaimed. "That's what I called Becky."

"I can't believe Becky," snorted Jodi. "She's such a creep. How dare she joke about your broken leg?"

"Jodi," I said. "She wasn't joking. That's what was *so* funny."

"Well, still," said Jodi, "it wasn't right."

Patrick was looking at me. I realized that he had been right. Jodi *was* still feeling guilty about my leg. I put my arm around her. "You know, Jodi, it wasn't your fault I broke my leg. Accidents happen. That's all it was."

Jodi looked relieved.

"Besides," I said, "it turned out it wasn't such a bad break after all."

"What do you mean?" asked Lauren. "It was a *bad* break. It hurt. You were out for a long time. You even thought of quitting."

"But I didn't quit," I said. "I learned a lot when I just started crying like a baby."

Darlene was staring at me. "Welcome to the human race, champ," she said softly.

"Thanks," I said.

"Cindi's not just human," said Ti An. "She's a Pinecone."

We all started to laugh, but I understood something now. There are worse things than being human. Maybe it took a bad break to teach me that. Some breaks aren't all bad.